The Adventures of Onyx
and
The Gales
of November

by Tyler Benson

Ensign Benson Books LLC

Ensign Benson Books LLC
PO BOX 609
Gloucester, VA 23061
www.adventuresofonyx.com
ensignbensonbooks@gmail.com

Printed and bound in the United States of America

First Edition

10 9 8 7 6 5 4 3

LCCN 2013937807

ISBN 978-0-9892846-0-8

book bridge press[sm]

This book was expertly produced by Book Bridge Press.
www.bookbridgepress.com

To my wife, Kristy. Thank you for your service, sacrifice, understanding, and unwavering support to me and our Coastie family! I thank God that he chose you to join me in my Coast Guard journey. I love you—let the adventures continue!

—Tyler

"Mayday, Mayday, Mayday!" The cry for help came across the radio in the communications center of Coast Guard Station St. Ignace.

Sellers, the communication watchstander, answered the call, "Vessel hailing Mayday, this is the United States Coast Guard, state your location and nature of distress!"

A scared voice came over the radio once again. "Mayday, Coast Guard, Mayday! We are a single-engine plane and we are going down. I repeat, we are going down in the Straits of Mackinac!"

The radio suddenly went silent, and the phones began ringing loudly. Chief Trib entered the communications center and began assisting Sellers with the calls. Phone call after phone call came in from witnesses who spotted a small plane crash on the backside of Mackinac Island.

Chief Trib pointed to Sellers and said, "Alert the crew! It's time to get to work." The search and rescue alarm sounded through the station. The crew rushed in to dress out into their search and rescue suits. They were briefed before they ran out the door and sprinted toward the motor lifeboat, ready to answer the call, ready to save lives in need. They are The Guardians of the Straits.

The Coasties rushed to their positions. Dean went topside to the driver's seat. Evans went below to fire up the engines. Pelkey took the stern line, and Hogan took the bow line.

Dean looked toward the navigator chair at their newest crewmember. "All right, girl," he said with a grin. "Hold on tight! We're setting out into these heavy winds. We're setting out into the Gales of November!"

Onyx looked forward. With a loud, confident bark, she let her crew know she was ready to go. Onyx was ready for another adventure!

"All right, clear all lines!" Dean yelled. "Coming up!"

Onyx and The Guardians of the Straits launched into action!

As the motor lifeboat headed into the Straits, Dean briefed the crew. "Listen up. These Gales of November have just proven that they are not only capable of pulling ships to the bottom of the lakes, but that they are also capable of pulling aircraft from the sky! There are reports that this plane went down on the east side of Mackinac Island, somewhere in front of Arch Rock. The good news is that Coast Guard Cutter Biscayne Bay is in the vicinity to assist us with the search. The bad news is getting to them. We have to go through Round Island Passage!"

"Oh no!" Evans cried. "Not the pass!"

"What is the pass?" Hogan asked Pelkey.

"It's a narrow passage between Round Island and Mackinac Island," Pelkey explained. "It's where Lake Huron and Lake Michigan come together, and in these Gales of November the two lakes collide and explode!"

"The risk is worth the gain!" Dean yelled. "It will cost us valuable time to go around Mackinac Island. Who's with me?"

Onyx barked first, then the crew shouted a united "Aye, aye!" The Guardians of the Straits would make the pass!

The motor lifeboat approached Round Island Passage. As the waves grew higher, the crew quickly buckled up and harnessed in.

Hogan strapped Onyx into her chair. "Okay, girl, hold on tight," he said. "Dean is one of the best boat drivers in the Coast Guard. He'll get us through the pass safely. I trust him." Hogan took his seat. Onyx looked over at Dean. She saw the same confidence in his eyes that she held in her heart. A purpose to serve, a purpose to protect, and a purpose to save those in need. Dean was their leader. He was always ready. He truly was *Semper Paratus.*

As the motor lifeboat came to the passage, Dean yelled out, "Hold on, shipmates! Coming up!" then he pushed the throttles down.

The motor lifeboat slammed its bow into the powerful waves. The crew lowered their heads and grabbed the rail. Dean held tightly onto the helm, and Onyx howled with exhilaration as the 40,000-pound motor lifeboat made its big push and leaped 30 feet into the air.

The motor lifeboat was airborne for seconds, but suddenly slammed down and rode the back of the wave. "Ha ha!" Dean yelled to the crew. "We made it!"

Onyx barked with excitement and licked Hogan's face. "I wasn't scared for a second," Hogan told Onyx.

Suddenly, Coast Guard Cutter Biscayne Bay came over the radio. "St. Ignace Rescue, we have visual on the plane crash. It's on the shore of Mackinac Island at the base of Arch Rock. It's too shallow for our cutter or your motor lifeboat to get in there. Request we launch our small boat to come alongside your boat to take one of your emergency medical technicians into the beach to assist. Air Station Traverse City has a rescue helicopter on the way."

"Hogan!" Dean yelled. "That is you! Prepare for transfer with Biscayne Bay's small boat, and take Onyx."

The small boat came alongside the motor lifeboat. Evans and Pelkey helped Onyx and Hogan across. "Good luck, shipmates!" Evans said.

Onyx barked and Hogan gave them a thumbs-up. Hogan and Onyx met their new crew. The Gibb twins! Hogan introduced himself and Onyx. "It's a surprise to see brothers stationed together!" Hogan yelled.

"As surprising as it is for us to see that your rescue party consists of a Coastie and a dog!" one of the brothers yelled back.

"She's as much of a Coastie as you or your brother. You just watch!" Hogan said.

The small boat headed for shore. Hogan and the Gibb twins held on tight, while Onyx stood as a watchful guardian at the bow. The small boat bounced from wave to wave, quickly making its way closer to the shore.

As they closed in on the beach, one of the Gibbs yelled out, "Brace yourselves!" The small boat suddenly hit bottom and beached itself onto Mackinac Island.

One Gibb brother grabbed the emergency medical kit. The other radioed back to the cutter and motor lifeboat about their arrival. Onyx wasted no time. She sprinted across the beach toward the flames and smoke of the plane crash. The dog led the way as the Coasties followed.

Onyx led the Coasties up the bluff to the base of Arch Rock where the aircraft lay. Wreckage from the plane paved the path all the way up to the bluff. Onyx and the Coasties worked their way through the debris and the brush of the island until they came across the fuselage of the plane, which holds the passengers, crew, and cargo.

Onyx started barking furiously, scraping her claws against the fogged-up window of the fuselage. One of the brothers yelled for her to get back. "No one could have survived that crash!" Hogan tried to pull the aircraft doors open, but the fuselage was too warped and too twisted to open.

Hogan ran back to the small boat, grabbed the boat's anchor, and then quickly sprinted back up the bluff toward the crash. He pushed the brothers aside and yelled to Onyx, "Get back!" Then he threw the anchor through the fogged window, shattering it to pieces.

To everyone's surprise, a badly injured woman emerged from the passenger seating and handed one of her three children to Hogan. "Save my children!" she said. "Save my children!" Hogan embraced the child against his chest. Onyx nuzzled against the mother to give her comfort.

Suddenly, Hogan and Onyx looked up to see the bottom of an orange Coast Guard rescue helicopter arriving from Air Station Traverse City. A basket from the rescue helicopter lowered, and a rescue swimmer stepped onto the bluff of Arch Rock.

"I'll take it from here," the swimmer told Hogan.

Hogan and the Gibb twins put the mother and her three children in the basket. Onyx ran up to the basket. The mother pulled Onyx close. "Thank you, miracle dog, thank you! You saved my babies and me," the mother whispered into Onyx's ear.

The helicopter began lifting the rescue basket. The mother held onto Onyx as long as she could, finally letting go as she and her children rose safely into the air.

Hogan kneeled next to Onyx with the Gibb brothers and watched, knowing that a family would safely see another day. Onyx stood proud knowing that she had found exactly what she was born to do. Serve and protect a greater good. Her perseverance paid off. Onyx survived another adventure—and the Gales of November.